THE PARABLE OF
SHELBY THE MAGNIFICENT

In Which the Windy Woods Campers Learn
the Biblical Value of Humility

By Michael Waite
Illustrated by Sheila Lucas

A person who is humble will be honored

Proverbs 29:23

Dear Parents: *Read* Shelby the Magnificent *aloud with your family. Talk about the story and what it means to be proud and to be humble. Discuss Proverbs 29:23 and memorize it together. The verse will serve as a reminder of the Christian value of humility.*

Be sure to look for these other Camp Windy Woods books and toys!

· Digger's Marvelous Moleberry Patch
· Lady Bug Island
· Butterflies for Two

· Bartholomew Beaver and the Stupendous Splash
· Daisy Doddlepaws and the Windy Woods Treasure
· Camp Windy Woods Peel and Play

Shelby Turtle tipped his hat and gave his cape a little swish as he watched himself in the mirror.

"For my first trick," he said to the mirror, "I shall put my toy hop-frog, Mr. Peeps, into the Astonishing Bag of Wonder and make him disappear!"

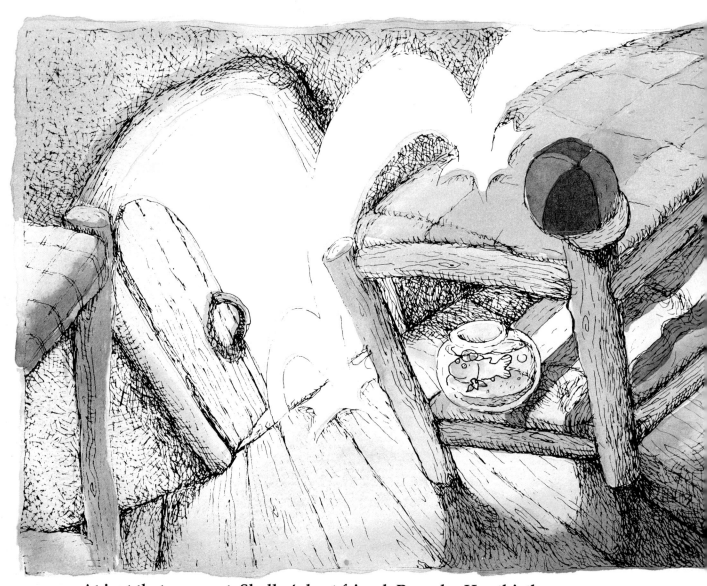

At just that moment, Shelby's best friend, Barnaby Hopthistle, came tumbling into the cabin. He pounced over a row of bunks and landed with a *thump* at Shelby's feet.

"Hullo!" he said, smiling up from the floor. "Say! That's a dandy costume you've got on!"

"Oh, is it really?" said Shelby, twirling round excitedly. "I'm practicing tricks so I can be in the Talent Show tomorrow. Watch this!"

He dropped Mr. Peeps into the Astonishing Bag of Wonder and tied it shut. Then he closed his eyes and scrunched up his face to concentrate.

5

"Winkus-Pinkus, Dippity-Doo!" he said in a squeaky voice. He tapped the bag with his wand. "Okey-doke! Now you can look inside."

Barnaby dug through the bag top to bottom.
"It's gone!" he gasped. "You made it disappear!"
"Ah-ha!" cried Shelby. And with a big swish of his cape, he swept off his hat. Out fell Mr. Peeps.

"Hooray!" cheered Barnaby. He bounced up and down on the bunk, clapping.

"Oh! You liked it?" cried Shelby. He flapped his cape excitedly. "I know more tricks too! Lots and lots! Do you really think I should be in the Talent Show?"

"Yes, yes!" cheered Barnaby. "And I can be your Assistant! Then you can put me in the Astonishing Bag of Wonder!"

"Uh-oh!" said Shelby, looking at his watch. "It's time for rehearsal! I'd better hurry!"

He scooped up his magic wand and the Astonishing Bag of Wonder, and trotted down the path toward the Little Stage in the Orchard. Barnaby skipped along beside him chattering away about Assistants and disappearing and things like that.

8

But Shelby wasn't really listening. He was thinking how wonderful it would feel to be up on stage, with everyone clapping and cheering! And as he hurried along, with his cape floating behind him and his tall hat sitting grandly on his head, he began to feel just like a real magician.

When they arrived at the Orchard, Lucy Goosefeathers was leaping around on the stage doing a tap dance song. Shelby watched for a little while. But then he started practicing with his magic wand. "Should I do little swirls and swishes?" he said to himself, wiggling it round in the air. "Or great big loopy-swoops?" He decided on great big loopy swoops, and forgot to clap when Lucy was finished.

After Lucy left the stage, Digger Mole got up and played something or other on his violin. And Daisy Doddlepaws tooted a funny little song on her tuba.

There were probably a couple plays and dances and that sort of thing, too, but Shelby really didn't notice. He was busy straightening his costume and practicing his loopy-swoops.

Then, just when Shelby thought it was going to be his turn, Blossom Sweetpaws stumbled onto the stage with an armful of bean bags, dropping them as she went. As soon as she started to juggle, bean bags flew everywhere. One hit Bartholomew Beaver on the nose, almost waking him up. Another landed inside Daisy Doddlepaws' tuba. And a third one hit Barnaby Hopthistle on the tail.

That was more than Shelby could take. "My Turtle tricks are too clever for *this* talent show!" he snorted. He jumped to his feet, gathered his cape around him, and hurried out of the Orchard. Barnaby scampered after him.

"I'm going to have my own Talent Show!" huffed Shelby. "Then I can have the whole stage all to myself. And pretty soon I'll be a World-Famous Magician. Don't you think so?"

"Uh-huh," said Barnaby, skipping on one foot, then the other. "And I can be your Assistant, who gets put in the Astonishing Bag of Wonder and disappears!"

So, they hurried back to Pondwater Cabin and made a big stack of posters. Then Barnaby ran all over Camp Windy Woods and tacked them up on trees.

Shelby went to the Orchard right after dinner to set up the stage. He could hardly wait for all the campers to come crowding in to see him! He was already beginning to feel like a World-Famous Magician.

But six o'clock came and went, and the seats in the Orchard were still empty. So Shelby sat down on the stage and waited.

He waited...

       and waited...

             and waited... while the moon climbed up to the clouds, and the air grew cold and damp, and night fell dark and silent.

"Where could everyone be?" he said gloomily, wrapping his cape around him in the cold.

"Maybe they all got lost," said Barnaby. "Or eaten up by Gobblums. I'd better go look for them just in case they didn't."

And he bounced off down the pathway, leaving Shelby all alone on the stage.

He sat there for a long, long while, growing madder and madder by the moment.

"A World-Famous Magician shouldn't have to sit and wait for people to come see his tricks!" he huffed at last. And he got up to leave.

But just as he came to the top of the stairs, he tripped on the end of his magic cape and went tumbling off the stage. He rolled across the path and landed in a thick patch of briars.

21

"Help!" he squealed. "Help! I'm stuck!"

And stuck he was! His magic cape had wrapped itself around him so tightly that he couldn't move so much as a finger. Every time he tried to wiggle himself loose, prickle bushes jabbed him in places he didn't wish to be jabbed, and bits of dust flew up his nose.

So there he stayed for a very long time with nothing to do but think.

And the longer he thought, the more he wondered whether he hadn't become a bit of a Proudy Pants lately.

"That's what it is," he moaned to himself, shamefully. "I've become a horrible Proudy Pants and that's why no one came to the show. I didn't clap at the rehearsal, or say nice things to anybody, or do anything but think of myself! And now look what it's all come to! I'll be wrapped up in this horrible magic cape forever and ever!"

He let out another moan, and just then, a yellow glow lit up the bushes.

Up the pathway came Uncle Beardsley and all of Shelby's friends!
Uncle Beardsley untangled him from the briars and helped straighten
his costume.

"Goodness, Shelby!" he said, wiping the twigs and dust away. "Are
you all right?"

"No," said Shelby, gloomily. He took off his magic cape and hat and handed them to Uncle Beardsley. "I wish I'd never tried to be Shelby the Magnificent. I only did it because I thought everyone would like me more. But instead I turned into a horrible Proudy Pants, and now nobody likes me at all!"

"I like you, Shelby!" said a little voice.

Shelby turned around to see where the voice had come from. But the only thing behind him was the Astonishing Bag of Wonder lying at the edge of the stage. Just then, it started to wiggle. Everyone backed away, and Blossom Sweetpaws let out a frightened squeak.

Then, suddenly,

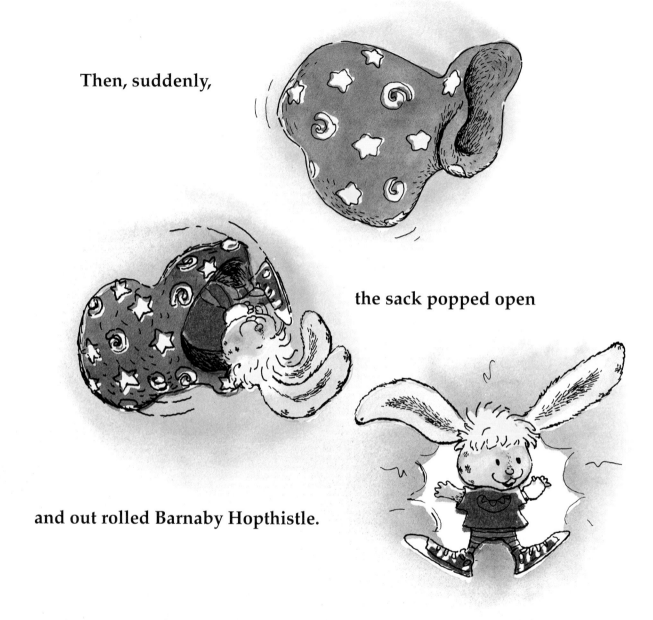

the sack popped open

and out rolled Barnaby Hopthistle.

"Barnaby!" cried Shelby, and he hugged his best friend.
"Besides," said Barnaby. "You're not a Proudy Pants *all* the time!"

Everyone laughed and hugged and said they were sorry. And even though it was long past Lights Out, Uncle Beardsley took them all back to the Cottage-by-the-Lake for hot cocoa and cookies.

If you had been passing through Camp Windy Woods that night, and you'd heard all the laughing and chatter, you could have peeked through the windows of the Cottage-by-the-Lake, and inside, you would have seen Shelby Turtle doing tricks for all his friends.

But this time, he wasn't Shelby the Magnificent, World-Famous Magician. He was just good old Shelby Turtle, the turtle everyone liked best.

THE HUMBLE SONG

A Camp Windy Woods Song
by Lucy Goosefeathers

Oh, I want to be a humble-bumble camper,
Humble through the dilly-dally day!
'Cause if I'm loud and proud,
I might attract a crowd,
But every friend I have will run away!

Oh, I want to be a humble-bumble camper,
Humble from my tootsies to my hair!
'Cause when I'm nice and humble,
I'm not so apt to stumble,
And my friends will always know how much I care!

Chariot Books™ is an imprint of Chariot Family Publishing
Cook Communications, Colorado Springs, CO 80918
Cook Communications, Paris, Ontario
Kingsway Communications, Eastbourne, England

SHELBY THE MAGNIFICENT
© 1996 by Michael Waite for text and Sheila Lucas for illustrations

Cover design by Michael Waite
Cover illustration by Sheila Lucas
First printing, 1996
Printed in Canada
00 99 98 97 96   5 4 3 2 1